SORCERESS
OF
ANGRA

JENNIFER TEIXEIRA

Sorceress of Angra

First paperback edition January 2022

ISBN 979-8-9855266-0-8 (paperback)

Dedicated to
Chase Goodman-Worthington

Thanks go to my Parents, Grandparents and Family, for their love of the islands and providing a safe place to land in the Atlantic. With special thanks to my mother, my sister Ariel, and my good friend Metzalli for their help and encouragement.

To my Amazon Blood Mothers who encouraged me to look into the divine feminine and bring this story to life as part of my legacy work with my ancestors and the Goddess Hekate.

Thank you to Jose *Leitão*, for all of his work and research on the Portuguese Inquisition.

Thank You to the Azores Islands Genealogy and DNA group I am part of for help in the research into the background of individuals in this story.

To all the murdered, tortured and persecuted souls whose stories have been immortalized by the Portuguese Inquisition. May you rest in Peace.

To my Teachers and Guides throughout my journey into Sorcery itself.

I give you my thanks.

Author's Note

The following tale is based on the author's research into the Portuguese Inquisition, her knowledge of sorcery and her familiarity with the Azores Islands, Portugal. There was one story that stood out, from all of the translations of the inquisitor's files from the islands. This is the story of the famed Sorceress of Angra; Barbara de Figueiredo. While the following story itself is a work of Historical fiction, the people, places, and many of the magical acts are as written in history by the inquisitors. This document has been translated, and applied into the story, so the reader can get a better idea at what it was like in the time of the inquisition in the Azores.

The Azores are comprised of 9 islands in the Macaronesian region of the Atlantic. The most western islands being Flores and Corvo, the middle grouping of islands are Graciosa, Terceira, São Jorge, Pico, and Faial, and the most Eastern Group is São Miguel and Santa Maria. The Azores islands are 870 mi west of Lisbon, about 930 mi northwest of Morocco, and about 1,200 mi southeast of Newfoundland, Canada. The Azores islands are an autonomous region in the country of Portugal.

It should be taken into account that the writings in this book are from the author's own perspective as a modern American woman with roots in the islands. There will be the author's own interpretation of signs, symbols and research within these pages. Just as you cannot fully describe the scenery of a place in mere words, you cannot fully understand all of the lore coming from this place, within a mere book. There is much to be said of the experience of each of the senses. The sight, smell, taste, feel, touch and extrasensory perception to the magic found within this land. Most of the folk magic traditions were never written down, and those practitioners of old would have tried to keep them hidden anyway. Since the Azores are a strategic point but also an isolated place within the Atlantic, There has been much transcultural influence. In researching this book, I got to talk to many people, and engage the memories of many of my elders. It was a connective activity that brought me closer to my roots, and gave me many questions.

It sometimes is necessary for people to learn of their culture and the culture of others through story. This is why I have framed this book in such a way, from the fictional perspective that utilizes historic and true events to embed a particular time and place into your mind. Though the story of Barbara is fiction, she was a real person who had influence in the community. Everything in this Novela has happened throughout history, though the characters may vary and the stories from different sources put it all into perspective. Many of the magical spells she has been documented as performing, can be looked at through the eyes of a modern witch, and translated for better understanding.

In my research on witchcraft and the Portuguese Inquisition particularly in the Azores islands, I have found a few names of people accused of various things by the Inquisition. Their so-called crimes were things like Witchcraft, Superstitious behavior, Curandera/Healings, Visions, Divination and Blasphemy against the Catholic Church. All of the people listed here are recorded as being accused of these so-called crimes and all were jailed for a period of time. Much of their records are documented by the Inquisitors, and are written in Portuguese, with many of the pages being very hard to read. It has been difficult to translate, though there are a few things I found out. The punishments for these crimes varied, and could be anything from having a " citra sanguinis effusionem" a controlled beating (not to draw blood), Public Humiliation via Auto-da-fe (translates to "Theatre of Faith") which is a public ritual of penance, that typically would be a parade of the accused organized by the severity of their crime, each individual would wear a "carocha" which was a penitential hat that would have illustrations of their crimes, each person would have to go to the front and state their crimes to the public and declare guilt. It would almost always include penitence, going back to Catholic school, sometimes exile (often to the colonies; most to Brazil, but some to the island of Principe and Cabo Verde) for a number of years, repayment of all the costs associated. The accused could be executed by hanging, but many of these people died in prison awaiting trial. These names are those from the Azores accused of the crimes listed above, but they do not include all of the people who came under attack from the church. Many people came to the Azores as "New Christians" and this could mean they were Jewish or Muslim before being converted. To be accused of Judaism usually carries the sentence of "having your bones burned to dust" .

These names each tell a story, they were once a living person who had dreams and sought to survive the best they could in this world. More information can be found at antt.dglab.gov.pt including photocopies of the original inquisitor's notes in Portuguese.

The Accused:

MARIANA DA COLUNA

She was A 22 year old Nun from Sao Miguel who was accused of Sorcery in 1633 and 1637AD.

JERÓNIMA DE SOUSA

She was A 70 year old woman from Sao Miguel. She was arrested in Ponta Delgada 1619-1621 accused of Witchcraft and Sorcery.

Her sentence included going to the "auto-da-fe" (a public ritual of penance) with a candle in hand and a carocha (A cap depicting your accusations) on the head, slight abjuration(solemn repudiation, abandonment, or renunciation by or upon oath, often the renunciation of witchcraft), The punishment of exile to Brazil for three years, instruction in the Catholic faith via imprisonment in Catholic School, spiritual penances, and repayment of costs likely through indentured servitude.

FRANCISCO

Francisco was a slave born of an African woman and was also said to be the son of Agostinho Zimbrão Borges. Many different sources confirm that Agostinho and Francisco's mother had been engaged in a sexual relationship and had a child together. In 1743 Francisco was accused of Sorcery in Angra, Terceira.

INÊS FRANCISCA DA COSTA

The year was 1790 in Franca do Campo on the island of São Miguel.
Inês Francisca da Costa
  is accused of Witchcraft and Sorcery.

PADRE FRANCISCO DE SANTA ROSA

This 28 year old priest of the Order of Sao Francisco from the island of Pico, Padre Francisco De Santa Rosa died while in prison (it is said to be of natural causes) who had been under trial accused of witchcraft and superstitious activity between the years of 1761-1762.

CATARINA BERNARDA DO SACRAMENTO

In 1792 she was accused of Witchcraft and Sorcery.

AMARO FERNANDES

In 1659 A 50 year old farmer from Agualva on Terceira Island was accused of divination, cures, and other revelations by the inquisition. He was convicted in 1660 and had a sentence including public humiliation, auto-da-fe, exile to Brazil for 5 years and a repayment of costs.

MATEUS VAZ

Between the years of 1711-1716 ~ This 25 year old man from Praia on Graciosa Island was accused of Superstitions and Witchcraft. He was convicted and his sentence included confiscation of all property, auto de fe, abjuration, prison, perpetual penitential habit, being publicly flogged, banishment for 5 years for the galleys (slavery) and spiritual penances.

BALTASAR GONÇALVES

Between the years of 1583-1584 a 50 year old Blacksmith from Angra, Terceira Island is accused of visions and revelations. He was eventually determined to be crazy and was not convicted and eventually released back to Terceira Island.

ANTÓNIO DE GOUVEIA

The accused is a 29 year old person from Praia, Terceira island who has been accused of curandera, healings, superstitions, and witchcraft. On 07/14/1561 They are found to be guilty by the Inquisitors and the sentence was thus; penance for heresy, with head uncovered and holding a lit candle in the hand with vehement public abjuration, sent to prison, suspension of orders and priestly office at will, not to do cures or use the office of priest again.

This defendant had fled from the prison of Colégio da Doctrina on 5/2/1564, was arrested again and sentenced in 1564 with exile to the galleys (slavery)

Because of an illness caused by the sun, (Unsure what this is) Antonio ran away again and walked through Italy, France, and Germany. At his request the penalty of the galleys was lifted and released from them. Antonio was allowed to go to Terceira Island on 11/18/1566, being unable to return to Lisbon. As he did not comply with the sentence, he was returned to prison on 8/26/1567 and sentenced on 10/17/1567, to two years of exile to Brazil and not to enter Lisbon again. He was what can be called a "cangaceiro" and has had some infamy in Brazil.

On 10/09/1571 he entered the prison of the Santo Ofício of Lisbon again, being chained in irons in a ship coming from Pernambuco, Brazil, there were serious accusations against him at the Inquisition table.

BÁRBARA DA CONCEIÇÃO

During the years of 1742-1743 Barbara from Sao Miguel Island was accused of superstitions and sorcery. Unfortunately she died in prison. 1743.

FRANCISCA DE OLIVEIRA

Between the years of 1792-1794 she was accused of superstitions and sorcery. She was from Sao Miguel Island.

AURÉLIA FELICIANA

A weaver from Terceira island who was accused of sorcery. Her sentence was a private auto-da-fe on 11/24/1792. She was admitted to the hospital Real de S. José for madness and was examined and approved insane by the medical professors.

SEBASTIÃO

Sebastião was A 20 year old former slave (was born into slavery and became free after a certain age) of Captain João Neto da Cunha from Graciosa island. He was accused and convicted of sorcery, his sentence came in 1692 and included being flogged in the streets, "citra sanguinis effusionem" (a controlled beating not to draw blood). Imprisonment at the discretion of inquisitors, schooling on Catholicism, banishment for 3 years to Castro Marim, penitence and payment of all costs.

PADRE FREI FRANCISCO DO ROSÁRIO

This was a 50 year old Priest from Praia da Vitória, Terceira Island but originally from Brazil who was accused of Blasphemy in 1781. His Sentence included; auto-da-fe, abjuration, deprived of an active and passive voice, forever, and the exercise of his orders, for five years, exile to Cape Verde, for five years, after this exile he was sent to the Lisbon prisons and then he would leave in exile to the most remote convent in his province, where he would stay. One year in prison in the same convent, that this same sentence would be read in the parish church of Vila da Praia on a festa day, by a notary of the Holy Office, and in the same way in the chapter of the convent where he was a resident, spiritual penalties and penances and ordinary instruction.

BEATRIZ DOS SANTOS

In 1637 Beatriz Dos Santos, also known as Beatriz Rodrigues from the island of Sao Miguel was accused of Sorcery. She was arrested and her sentence included Catholic School, Spiritual Penances, Public Flogging in the Streets of Lisbon. "citra sanguinis efesionem" (controlled beating, not to draw blood). She was to be exiled to the island of Principe for 10 Years.

MANUEL CORREIA

Manuel Correia was a 40 year old man from Sao Miguel and he was described as a "Poor Man" and "Beggar" . He was accused of Sorcery in 1731 and was convicted with the sentence including; Catholic School, Being dragged through the streets with the label of "Sorcerer" with further humiliation of being exiled from entering Eastern and Western Lisbon.

SUSANA JORGE

In 1620, the 40 year old Susana Jorge who was from Sao Miguel island was accused of witchcraft and Sorcery. Her sentence included being whipped in public, "Spiritual penances" Exile to Brazil for 10 years and repayment of all costs.

MARIA DO ROSÁRIO E ANA JOAQUINA

In 1793 these two women from Angra, Terceira were accused of Superstitious behavior

BARBARA DE FIGUEIRIDO

CHAPTER 1

The Visitor

The sea tossed around the little boat as though it was a new baby among aunties. It lurched forward, leaping the waves and then disappearing, somehow managing to pop back up again.

But for every small sense of progress, the angry waves only pushed it back twice as far, with the result that most of the time, it was heading backward again, toward where it had come from.

The men were determined to carry on anyway, relentless, keeping on pushing the boat forward toward its destination as best they were able. But the truth was that they were not able at all; they were no match for the wrath of the ocean and its writhing depths.

No man could ever be a match.

Only they had not realized it yet.

The waves forever sought to challenge them and test their might, but as was the way with most men, they already believed they were its masters, able to command a vessel wherever they willed it to go. They could not. Their human arrogance had possessed their minds, filling their heads with the misguided notion that they could sail to wherever they wished. Of course, they had heard of other mortal men doing it and surviving, and landing ashore wherever they pleased.

The sea, especially on a wild night, had other ideas.

And woe betide the man who defied it, believing he could beat the sea at its own game. But there was more to the watery depths than met the eye. If you chose to look into the churning sea, you would risk becoming lost in it, taken down to an unknown world beyond the waves. It was like the iceberg that showed a tiny fragment of itself above the water, hiding its real self under the ocean. So too Isabel would experience how it was to become consumed by the sea.

***

Isabel had recently traveled by boat for a number of days and nights, her destination the island of Terceira. Here, she was set on meeting up with the famed healer, Barbara, someone she could not see anywhere else. Not only did she wish to have more opportunity in the active city, but also, Isabel had come here to study the healing work and open body mediumship for which Barbara was most famous. Who would be better to assist her than Barbara? Everyone knew she was the best.

There was nobody else she would ever dream of seeing.

For sure, Barbara would be the one to help her, to assist her closer to her aspirations.

In the city of Angra, she longed for connection to the people, for opportunities not available to those in the secluded villages of distant islands. There was never a shortage of people coming from all over for wishes granted by Barbara, and her fame had begun to spread throughout the islands for her knowledge of sorcery and healing work.

Somehow, the little boat that carried Isabel closer to Barbara finally made it to its destination, and it was a glorious night when it sailed into the harbor. As it eventually drew close to the Pier in Terceira, the beauty of the Church of Mercy and all the lights of the city, an amazing spectacle she had never witnessed before. It was as though the whole of Terceira had chosen to welcome her—though of course, they had not. But the tiny glowing lights seemed so welcoming, as if they cried out, *see, you have come, Isabel! Welcome, Isabel—we are so full of joy to see you here!*

Indeed, there were so many lamplights and streets that the city looked like a spiderweb, the pinpricks of light resembling sparkling dew in a morning mist.

The boat came into dock and found itself moored and still, its many passengers being led off it and into the city. Isabel was relieved to set foot on this solid ground at last. Her balance had been terribly affected by the constant *up, down, up, down* of the rolling sea that she could barely stand straight by the time she hit land. It was a blessed relief to not have to set foot on a boat again.

At least, not right now.

So, her feet dizzy from the lurching boat, and her mind spinning from dehydration, she was sure she would come to dream of the dead walking through the waves tonight.

She had only a short walk uphill to find Barbara's home, following the vague description the woman had given her. Isabel had tried to draw herself a map, only drawing was not her best point—just like sailing—and now, she turned the map this way and that, trying to see which way up it was supposed to go. But the city of Angra was small and surely, almost anyone knew where Barbara lived.

She stopped and asked a merchant who was closing up his storefront.

"Excuse me. I am so sorry to trouble you. I am looking for—"

"*Barbara,*" he completed. "So, show me someone who is *not* looking for Barbara and I will show you a miracle. Whatever this Barbara has, I wish I possessed it, for then I would be sure to earn a fat income. This store brings me almost nothing—yet every day, I hear *Barbara, Barbara!*"

Despite the man's dour attitude and bad mood, he told Isabel how to find the place.

And soon enough, after she had trekked up a steep cobbled hill and down the other side, and turned left by the small fig tree just as the man had said, she came upon Barbara's home on the right hand side. Above the door, a small white sign had been nailed, handwritten.

The home of Barbara.

It was an attached stone cottage, one with a low doorframe that even the shortest person would have to bend their neck just a bit to get through. She laid her hands on the stone just around the door. It felt cold and wet, and oddly so, as it was not even an especially chilly or damp day.

These old structures were said to hold on to the tales and happenings of times past, however.

This one had seen many a century pass it by—many a century being lived beneath its roof and between its walls. As Isabel knew, it was already casting off its vibrations of all the stories of the many who had lived here, whose souls had never quite known how to depart.

The stone surely held onto the tales of the plague, of the loneliness of death that eventually made its home in every heart. Isabel swore she could sense the writhing and tortured deaths of the many as they huddled in cold beneath their itching woolen blankets, miserable, waiting to pass to the next plane. She could feel the aching loss of a child, its death being brought into the world.

Or of a mother whose son had never come home from a voyage, and who'd stood at the tiny cottage windows for weeks on end, looking and waiting. The stone held onto them all—all the tales, all the experiences, all the happy times and the countless sad ones too. But more the sad…

The stone, too, had been worn down with time, as though even the cottage was feeling weary.

Isabel gently touched her fingertips across its surface by the doorway, feeling a tingle of the familiar volcanic rock, just like her own back home. She knocked gently on the wooden door, still dizzy from being brought in on the tumultuous waves. At one stage, she almost stumbled and caught herself, not wanting the city dwellers to see her looking as though she had just come home from a night at the alehouse. People gossiped aplenty in these small places.

She had no inclination to add to it by giving them food for their idle chatter.

Someone inside had heard Isabel's timid knock. Footsteps *clack-clacked* along a tiled floor.

The door opened a crack and from within, a young woman with freckled skin, dark eyes and long dark hair tied up under a bright spotted kerchief peeked outside to answer.

"Yes? What can I do for you?"

She was pretty, with the kind of unblemished pallor that could only come from living in fresh air—or perhaps from never seeing outside at all. Either was possible.

"Hello, I am Isabel from Pico…" Isabel said with a pause. "I've come to see—"

"Ah! Then you are surely *the* Isabel." replied the dark-eyed woman.

There was no smile crossing her face, but no scowl either.

She looked more inquisitive and eager for an answer. But also a little tired, perhaps.

"Yes! Yes! That is me, Isabel from Pico. Barbara is expecting me."

A faint smile did cross the woman's demeanor at this point.

"Oh, hello, I am Barbara's niece, Maria. It's so good to meet you, Isabel. Come inside and have something to eat, you must be hungry! Look at you—there is almost nothing to you!"

She lightly pinched at Isabel's arm with a grin, the way a hungry leper must have done to plump children in the scary stories she was told as a child. It sent a small shudder through the visitor.

But she had no other bad thoughts.

It had only been an old wives tale, after all. Isabel would soon be able to make her own stories here in this place. Nice stories. None of visitors being locked up by wicked lepers, and then eaten!

Maria led Isabel down the long dark hallway and out through a ramshackle low doorway to the back patio, where Barbara had been at her outdoor hearth preparing bacalhau for dinner.

It was a dish of salted codfish, potatoes and collards, popular all over the islands.

"Welcome! Welcome! God has blessed us with you. Come! Sit and join us for a meal."

Barbara patted at a thick padded seat on a long wooden bench that would seat two.

She appeared overjoyed at having a new guest, one who was so eager to learn and who hopefully had the aptitude for it as well.

Isabel somewhat underestimated herself in that regard, since just as Isabel had heard much about Barbara, so too had Barbara long since been hearing good things about young Isabel. Her reputation preceded her, in a positive way.

She had some fame around her just the same way Barbara did, having been gifted with mediumship, oneiromancy and clairaudience. People said that in her dreams, she spoke to the dead and in turn, the dead spoke to her in her waking hours. Barbara was keen to find out if it was true.

Isabel had been thinking about contacting Barbara for quite some time now. She needed her advice and help, and she was becoming more desperate for it as the days went by.

The town messenger had luckily been able to connect them, a joyous event for both women.

But of course, while it was the case that both could learn from the other, it was young Isabel who needed Barbara more. Things were difficult for Isabel lately.

She had begun feeling pursued.

***

In truth, while it was oftentimes a blessed gift to be able to commune with the dead, the poor departed souls did not always realize that it was supposed to be on Isabel's own terms, not just whenever and however they chose to pop by. Some were like an obnoxious relative who never stopped visiting and who outstayed their welcome on every visit, poking their noses in everything and giving the household no peace and no privacy. Some felt like an unwelcome invasion.

So, she sought out the advice of Barbara to help stop—or at least to curtail or control—these too frequent visions and intrusions. If she could only allow them at certain times and prevent them at others, she would be much happier. But right now, it felt as though she was being bothered wherever she went, and no matter what she was doing or trying to do in her life.

This much intrusion was unwelcome.

It was not what she had 'signed up for' so to speak. At night, the visions and awakenings robbed her of much-needed rest, sending her into the next day short-tempered and muddle-headed.

By day, she sometimes had other things to think about or with which to occupy herself, but the impertinent specters—as she sometimes thought of them—were always hanging around, asking for her company, her succor, her presence, her listening, her help to do something or other.

Dear Barbara, the spirits of the dead do not leave me alone!

What can I do? How do I stop them coming? she had sat and written *Can you give me guidance? I hear you have mastered them.*

Barbara's response by messenger was irksome. But still, Isabel took it all in.

My dear Isabel,

Thank you for your letter. But I am afraid you cannot 'stop them coming', as you put it.

Or should I say, you should not try to. Instead, you ought to invite them!

And you are not quite correct when you say I 'have mastered them'. My dear, it would be more accurate to say they have mastered me—or we have mastered each other.

We live in something akin to harmony.

But I can no more master them than you could train and master savage lions.

Best wishes,

Barbara.

Isabel was perplexed.

Invite them? What? Lions? Is this woman losing her mind?

So, maybe she should make up a spare bedroom for her guest spirits and lay extra places at the supper table too? Should she call them by name and tell them to come and go as they please?

If she had wanted to do that, she would have opened an inn that kept its doors open all day and all night, advertising, *come in and help yourself, anytime!*

What on earth was Barbara thinking?

But she was supposed to be the expert in all this, after all.

So Isabel thought she had better open up her ears and listen to her advice even if she hated it.

Dear Barbara, she had written one day.

I thank you for the blessing of your kind and gracious advice but I confess it does trouble and confound me. If I invite them in, will they not take advantage of my youth and my inexperience? Will they not drain me of my vitality and be even harder to send away?

Will I ever get time to myself when I need to be alone?

Yours fondly,

Isabel.

Well, Barbara also was perplexed. The girl Isabel seemed to believe the 'guests' were a problem bigger than she could handle. But really, there was nothing to it.

Sending letters to and fro was all well and good but there was no way to really help Isabel with the extent of her issues while she was at a distance. So, she sat and wrote again.

This time, she invited Isabel to her home to learn more about this skill.

Isabel, on receipt of this invitation, was overcome with joy.

Not only was Isabel excited to learn more, but a change of pace from her own village seemed like a positive step for her at this stage in life. She had always been in one place, and it was a small village, dull at times. Being able to travel and spend time with the famed Barbara was a dream come true. She was determined to make the most of it.

Isabel was no more than sixteen, but in these days, a woman at this age—and she *was* considered a woman already, not a child—was supposed to be thinking of marriage, and if not marriage, then she ought to be getting betrothed another way, by giving herself to God, as a nun.

Isabel had no interest in any of this. There was no time to waste before people would begin to talk. She simply wished to learn, and it was difficult for any woman to get a leg up in this world. Being invited to Barbara's side was such a gift.

Maybe Barbara herself had been sent by God? Who could say?

Maybe it was her own calling to talk with the dead, and Barbara would soon be able to show her a healthy way to make the most of all her unusual gifts and talents.

Barbara summoned Maria to bring the food to the table and make it ready for their guest.

As Maria was doing so, a frantic pounding came to the door, one that startled all in the home. Maria jumped up to make her way to answer it when a large woman holding up an equally large man pushed their way through. The man was breathing hard and red-faced. Sweat dripped copiously from his face and chin, like a rivulet that had no beginning and no end.

"Barbara, Barbara," the man pleaded, breathless and overcome by tearfulness. "Barbara, oh my God, save me. If you cannot save me, there is… no one who can."

Tears ran down his face and he was not ashamed by them.

"His wound is not healing, and his whole body feels hot to the touch! It has come over him all of a sudden! I dressed his wound last night when we went to bed. And then he was up all night, restless, screaming with the pain, Barbara. Can you help us?"

The woman said held onto the man who looked as though he could barely walk.

"Take a look. Dear," instructed Barbara, as though Isabel was already a fine apprentice well into the throes of learning. So, Isabel was the first to stoop and looked at his leg, and she saw the bloody bandage wrapped around the wound.

"This…is this the same bandage that you wrapped around his leg last night? Was it clean and fresh when you applied it?"

She held up the bandage between forefinger and thumb, dangling it, her face screwed up. Her expression said, *look at this disgusting thing.*

She tried hard not to sound accusatory. But somehow, she still did.

"No. It is the only bandage we have," said the woman. "We are poor. I rinse it through in the stream and dry it in the day. Then at night, we put it on again when it is dry. Or nearly dry. It depends on the weather. It seemed to be fine until yesterday."

"I mean, it looks…terrible," Isabel said. "See. It is so slimy. And smells so bad. You cannot just rinse it through like that. It will be filled with the essence of vileness that has now crept inside his skin. You are poisoning him. And don't ever reapply it when it is damp because—"

"Isabel, that's quite enough," Barbara said and frowned, displeased at the harsh and unkind words. The people around here often had no choices.

And they also had no knowledge of health matters. The woman had done her best.

And of course, the woman did not even need telling. She already suspected all that. But if her husband went to bed with the wound uncovered, the coarse and itchy blankets would chafe it raw. So, all they had was that wretched bandage to cover it with. First thing each morning, she whipped it off and went to wash it as best she was able. But the household also had no soap.

Isabel was not sure if it was the wound or the stress sweat that came out of his pores, but one way or the other, he stank to high heaven. She lay the supposed bandage on the ground and eyed Barbara with a look that said, *I don't know what else to say. This is revolting!*

Barbara came forward and inspected the wound.

"The girl is quite right," she said, "Though admittedly, I might have put it in slightly more delicate terms. I can see how you have been doing your best, and we only have what we have, my dear," she said to the wife. "No woman can work miracles with a single bandage."

Meanwhile, the husband was in agony, intermittently leaning on the wall for support.

"Can you assist me? Can you help?" he asked, moaning in agony.

He periodically lifted the leg like a horse waiting to be shod.

"Yes, that I can do," assured Barbara with a big smile. "Don't fret. It is not so far gone that we cannot save it. But like my young helper here said, the wound has become infected," Barbara proclaimed. "It is festering, and needs to be cleaned as a matter of some urgency."

She turned back to the wife who stood by in a state of fluster and panic.

"You can clean it for us?" she begged. "I can give you whatever money we have. Though it is not much."

She rummaged in the front pocket of her apron.

"Very well, I will take your coins," said Barbara. She extended her hand and the woman dropped in a single small silver, enough to buy some flour or a small chunk of cheese.

"I have no more," she said. She turned out her pocket. "I am sorry. I thought I had—"

Barbara felt in her own pocket and then extended a hand back to the wife, who seemed confused but reached out regardless. "What is this?" she asked, eyeing what Barbara had just dropped into her palm. There were now several silvers.

"Coins, like goodwill and rabbits, tend to multiply," she said with a laugh. "Here. Consider these my gift to you and your family. With these coins, you must do as I say. You chose to give your one coin to me, and I have learned that when someone gives to you, you must give back at least threefold. So that is what I choose to do. Put them in your apron."

The woman's eyes were wide, not believing her good fortune.

"Thank you, Miss Barbara. Thank you so much. How can I ever repay you?" Her voice was tearful now. "Of course, I will—we will—do with these whatever you command us to do."

"I know you will, dear. And what I command you to do is to purchase decent bandages,

"Those, you need not pay for as I have always bandages set aside. I use them for my poultices. You will remember to do that? You will then have at least ten feet of new white bandages for your husband. Throw away every soiled one and start again with new, and do it several times daily. And when you are out of new bandages, come back and see me and I will inspect the leg again."

"I am so grateful to you, Barbara. So very happy. I can do that—I will go fetch the bandages as soon as we leave here. But then what are the coins for?"

"The coins, my dear, are for you to buy a chicken and some vegetables, and a loaf of bread, some salt and seaweed, and whatever else you need. And with the chicken and the greens, you make your husband a healthy fat broth for tonight and tomorrow, you understand? Add butter for the fat. It helps him to heal. With the salt and the seaweed, you bathe his leg every hour. And buy sugar. New shoes for you both too, and undergarments, as I swear the winter is coming with a vengeance."

The woman simply burst into tears, rushing forward to clasp Barbara in her arms.

"I thank you, I thank you, I thank you!"

The man broke down in tears too. Meanwhile, however, his bad leg throbbed all the more. "You can clean my leg for me here?" he asked. "Is that too much to hope for?"

"Oh, We can do that here and now. My young friend shall help me again. These old bandages will rot his flesh, so they need to be burned. We will do that too, so you take home nothing dirty."

They will rot his flesh? Thought Isabel. *They already did!*

"Maria, Get some water to boil and place in as many malva leaves as will fit into a cup of the boiling water. Isabel, Gather a basin of cold water from the back and bring it in here. *Hurry up!*"

Barbara delegated, commanding the women around as if she were in charge of an army.

She instantly reached for a bottle of Aguardente sitting on the front table.

She had already steeped garlic, rosemary and thyme into the Aguardente, the herbs giving it a dark color, a strong flavor, and a very pungent aroma—though it was not unpleasant.

She poured out a generous cupful for the man to drink.

There was no better liquor for pain relief, and this would help with the pain and assist in clearing the infection by circulating in his blood quite soon.

"Here, sit down and drink this." He did it without question and soon found himself more relaxed, even giving the women a sheepish smile. "My ladies," he said. "My saviors, all."

Isabel was coming down the hallway with a large basin filled with clean rainwater.

Barbara met her as she came to the opening in the entranceway. She took a hold of the basin from Isabel and then placed the basin back on the floor by the seated man.

Isabel came and poured the rest of the bottle of Aguardente into the water.

"We start learning fast around here, huh Isabel?" Barbara said as she hurried to the man's legs and continued to unwrap the bandages, revealing a angry gaping and suppurating wound.

"How did this happen?" Barbara asked the man

" I slipped with an ax. Brought it down on my leg, chopping the wood for the fire. It hasn't healed, it hurts something terrible, and it's only gotten worse. It's been almost two weeks," the man replied, wincing. "It went in an inch. I was lucky not to take the whole goddamn leg off."

"Yes, I can see it is an old wound, this was not properly cared for. You should have come to me right away."

"We did not want to bother you, Barbara," said the wife, peering over to see what was being done for her husband, hoping to learn a little from Barbara's ministrations. "We hear how so many people come to trouble you. I said to my husband that we would try to make do."

"This is not a *make do* situation," admonished Barbara. "It is a deep cut. And what about the firewood?" she asked. "Don't tell me you also are in the cold without a way to cook your food?"

"We are in the cold," admitted the man. "*She* can't chop. And now, neither can I."

"Well, I shall have you back to it soon," Barbara said. "Meanwhile, I will send the girl over with plenty of chopped wood. We have more than enough."

Isabel winced now. Which of them—Maria or herself—was Barbara calling *the girl?*

Normally, she would think it was very rude. But somehow, she quashed her sense of offense. Coming from Barbara, it didn't sound so bad. Maybe by being *the girl,* she could learn a lot.

Barbara brought the man's feet into the water and gently washed the wound, removing pus and dirt that had found its way into the cut.

Maria came in with the hot malva leaves and she set them aside for Barbara.

Barbara took the leaves out of the hot water with her bare hands tempered by years of cooking and making up hot poultices from a myriad raw ingredients.

Then she mixed the hot water with the water in the basin and continued to wash the man's feet and legs. When the man was fully relaxed, she brought out her curved needle. She boiled it in water on the stove, then waited for it to cool. "Maria, fetch my thread box," she said.

Maria returned with sewing threads. "Which color would you like?" she teased the patient.

"Anything but red or black," he said, laughing for the first time. "Red reminds me of blood. Black reminds me of the parts that turned septic. Perhaps the white? To match the bandage."

"White it is, my good man," said Barbara. "Now, you know this will hurt, don't you? How about another shot of Aguardente first?"

She poured some into a small glass and he downed it in one.

Then he pursed his lips. "Here we go," she said, and began to sew the horrific wound shut.

The man grimaced at the needle, but found he could withstand the pain. His face told a story of trust and faith in what Barbara was doing. She was a skilled healer and would only help him.

When she was done, she placed the warm leaves over the wound and gently wrapped them with long strips of fabric.

"Maria, go fetch me my papers please."

Barbara was referring to her *cartas de tocar* or touching cards, small pieces of paper with beautiful prayers written on them and images of Christ on the cross.

They were used as a preventative, kept alongside a person to bless them with good luck and health. They held a special meaning for Barbara as they had been prepared for her own work in healing others. Many of Barbara's touching cards were very old, and their writings in Latin. They were a very special set with much meaning attached, given to her by the Priest João Cardoso, a close friend of hers. The prayers on them when read out loud would encourage blessings to all whose ears they touched, and so Barbara gave a voice to them out loud with confidence.

Even a stranger to the papers could not avoid feeling overwhelmed by their beauty and reverence, by their delicate and perfect images and their beautiful, reassuring words.

So Barbara did her work as if in a trance, adding her own blessings for healing as she continued to do her work. Isabel and Maria looked on, absorbing every prayer and incantation that came from her lips to help heal this man.

Finally when she was done, she looked up at him, holding his hand. He was sweating less from infection, but his face was wet anyway—this time, overcome by tears.

He cried as though he might not manage to stop, so touched was he.

"This wound needs to remain clean and the dressings changed as I mentioned. Let the leaves do their work till the sun comes up tomorrow," Barbara instructed. "You need even more time to heal, so give yourself time to rest. Take the leaves off in the morning. Do not soak them to remove them unless they have adhered themselves to the flesh and will not come free.

"In that case, bathe carefully and only with boiled water and new bandages. Allow the wound to be fully dry before you cover it. Do not expose the wound to filth or dirty fingertips. Let me wrap it again the next day if you need help."

The pair nodded in great gratitude and relief. The man already looked so much better and when he stood, he said, "The leg isn't even throbbing now. Kind of a dull pain. Leaf magic and tender hands have done the trick."

Everyone laughed.

The man nodded gratefully a final time, applied weight to the leg quite happily, and with only a slight hobble, he stepped out the front door with his good wife who also had a spring in her step.

***

"There is some mess here, and it needs to be cleaned up before we can eat. Maria, show Isabel what to do. She needs to get herself acquainted with this part of the work as it is a foundation to what we do here," Barbara said as she took a bottle from the cupboard.

She poured herself a cupful of wine. "Then we will eat."

"Isabel, so… we keep this space clean. The good spirits love a clean home and will visit us more often if we keep it so," Maria began as Barbara sat in the chair next in the foyer of the hall.

"We have vinegar soaked with bitter orange peels prepared every month for just this occasion. Make sure to wipe the floors and walls down in this room where the visitors came in. We can't allow their disease to stick here so we need to clean everything." Maria grabbed a small cloth along with a cup of bitter orange-peel-soaked vinegar from the shelf.

She handed them to Isabel.

"Evil will not enter a clean home," Barbara said. "Our work here keeps the place free of it."

"I will get the dry thyme and rosemary to fumigate the area as you work," Maria replied.

And with that, the two young women began to clean and build up their appetite for dinner once again. Barbara finished her wine and moved herself into the backyard to finish with the table setup.

Dinner was very simple, but it was fulfilling and the chatter after the events of the night brought the women together.

Once they had finished, Barbara led Isabel to her room.

"It is just us for now. My husband has been out to sea for some time, but he eventually does return. Well, let us at least hope so. There is a lock on the inside of the door if you feel you need it. I will be here if you need anything else," Barbara said with exhaustion. "Goodnight, Isabel."

CHAPTER 2

Mother God

B arbara was touched by the divine and had a gift for medium-ship, healing and sorcery, skills she had been gifted, but had nevertheless developed and honed over time.

She could be found in church every day with her devotions, as well as in her home, praying every morning when she woke and every night before she slept.

She was known for her healing powers as well as for what was known as *coscinomancy* or sieve divination. More than this, she was reputed to have a special gift for saving children from death. But this was a time in which everything was seen in polarity. Notably, that there was good and there was bad. People believed that to have great good, terrible evils also must exist.

There also were rumors of Barbara's ability to kill with sorcery as well as to heal, but her efforts seemed miraculous to the people, and she offered her mysterious powers to rich and poor alike.

***

After some months in her company and instruction, Isabel had witnessed first-hand the healing power of Barbara. The man with the ax cut had indeed healed. Not only that but he was doing much better than before, ending up stronger than before his terrible and life-threatening injury.

It was a miracle, people said. Every person in need looked up to Barbara.

In time, Isabel was able to witness Barbara's miraculous work as a midwife as well.

Barbara had come to the aid of many women in labor, some more difficult than others. In one instance, she was called upon in the middle of the night to come to a particularly difficult birth.

The mother was exhausted and had lost hope of ever seeing her newborn alive.

Barbara had carefully placed wet fabric around the mother's belly and face to help calm her, instructing the woman to drink the tea she had prepared just for her. Even the mere presence of Barbara had a relaxant effect; the women had trust in her abilities to do amazing and wondrous things. Was she aided by God himself? Did she only have to ask, and a healing would happen?

That was how it seemed sometimes. But not everything went so easily.

Soon, the woman's baby came out with so much force that when Barbara was able to see the baby, and hold it, the child was black and blue. He was not breathing and the mother cried out at the presumed death of her child who looked like a tiny corpse already. But Barbara moved quickly and began to briskly massage the child with circular fast motions, a mumbled prayer coming from her lips. She reached into his mouth with her smallest finger to pull out the obstruction.

Next, she laid him on the floor in front of the fire and gave the child her own breath to open up the lungs. Then, she held him upside down, slapping at his back.

Soon, through much effort and repeated attempts, the child awoke and let out a cry that cut through the sadness of death in the room. To the astonishment of the family, the newborn child wailed as if furious about his welcome into the world. He certainly had a lot to say!

Everyone was agog. They smiled until their faces hurt, and word spread that yet again, Barbara had worked her magic at a house of death, bringing a dead body back into the living world.

Barbara was immediately propelled as a holy woman who could bring the dead back to the realm of those who breathed. Women began to look to her for help when it came time for them to give birth, and soon, she had to chalk her appointments upon the kitchen wall with a stone, to remember all the things she had promised and the people to who she had promised them all.

People of villages near and far looked to Barbara for her wisdom and expertise as a healer, a sorcerer, and as a woman capable of giving new birth to those already departed for the next plane.

The next morning after the successful but traumatic birth, Barbara gathered her two apprentices for a walk to the holy mound that looked over all of the city of Angra.

This was a shifting point for Barbara. While she had been well known as a healer before, after this event with the resurrected child, she would have even more respect and legitimacy. There were always babies to be born, so there would always be a long line of women desperate for help.

Having her apprentices at her side was of great advantage. On her own, no way could Barbara, even as capable as she was, manage to save and assist so many with such varying ailments and problems. The young apprentices were eager and keen to do all they could. It was the only way to pick up the skills. Besides, who would not love to assist in bringing babies to this world?

It gave them a connection to something so precious, the gift that they could be so privileged to witness such a miracle. The three of them were now connected through this holy miracle. It was something that they could tell their children, and their children's children.

Barbara, Maria and Isabel walked arm in arm up the steep hill above the city, eventually stepping foot onto the land comprising the ruins of Castle of Moinhos. The irrigation system that provided water to the crops and people below stood out, with its pools and statuary. The hill was dotted with windmills, and the walls of the old medieval fort told a story of times long gone.

In her early years, Barbara had studied with a lay religious order known as the Beguines; there, she had received much instruction on the healing powers of herbs, midwifery, caring for the dead, and the art of working in wool and dye. These were all skills new to her. Many considered that Barbara had simply been born blessed and with the innate ability to know everything about everything. But she had not. She had been given an *aptitude,* and was always keen to learn more.

As a child, she had immersed herself in learning all that she could, learning from elders, and practicing her skills with wild plants and natural medicinal herbs.

But the Beguines had offered real learning, something she would always be grateful for.

These independent religious women had come to the Azores for some form of freedom to practice their ways of life. This was often through honoring the divine feminine that made itself manifest in their work, and by seeking knowledge of the meaning of life through the love of God.

They were among the few women in those days who could read and write, and because of this, often were suspected of practicing witchcraft themselves. This could not be further from the truth, as these women helped to form the religious path of the Azores and the Cult of the Holy Spirit.

They once brought Barbara to this place where she could see the mountain, and there they told her the story of Mother God. In turn, Barbara brought the two young women, Maria and Isabel to this place to lay eyes on her for themselves and to share in her beauty and wonder.

"Look toward the city and bring your eyes to the volcano directly across from us here," Barbara said proudly as she gazed at the mountain across the bay of Angra that sat above the city.

"Do you see Her?" Barbara asked as she turned her gaze to the women with her.

"There is no one there? I see the mountain only…" Maria replied. "I mean, that's all there is."

"You may well see the mountain, but do you not also see *Her* in the mountain? I had been on this hill gazing out for years and also never saw anything but a hillside, until these women told me what to look for," Barbara said. "And then I saw Her, as plain as I see you now.

"This place once served to help defend the city below, with its windmills and farms. It is the highest point in the city, overlooking the harbor and ocean, the valley and river below. One has a vantage point from this place, and you can be closest to the sky when you are over the city of Angra," Barbara said as her eyes filled with tears.

The most influential view was that of Monte Brasil.

When she looked past the stain of the Spanish fortress that had defiled the landscape of the mountain, she would envision Our Lady who had given birth to God.

"The fertile green mountain is a vision of Mother God. In this place, you witness the belly of the mountain reaching up to the sky, pregnant and full, ready to erupt as her legs spread out and toward the ocean, She who gives birth to the world," Barbara told them. "This is a living manifestation of Mother God, an image representing creation. I often come to this place and think of my mother, and of my role as midwife to many of the mothers in the city below."

The two young women nodded, unused to hearing Barbara tell them so much all at once.

She was so animated about this place, and enamored. And she had more to say yet.

"My life as a midwife was not chosen by me, but rather was ordained on me by the grace of God. When you have gifts such as we do, Maria and Isabel, then we need to use these gifts to take care of the mothers and children of this land and provide them with safety and health. The gifts we have been given are not rare, getting messages from the dead and the otherworld and God is much more common than one would think. It is the gathering of us here, together, to train and build ourselves from these gifts.- That is the rarity of it. Creating more from what we have initially been given. That is what makes us special."

"And you will note I talk of the mothers. Especially these must we take great care of. To do anything other than this would be sinful. It would mean we were being disrespectful of our God-given gifts, misusing them. God delivers gifts to us—or not—with His infinite wisdom.

"Men also do not know the ways of nurturing as we do," Barbara continued. "Women offer help to the people and give to the Church for many reasons, giving freely of our hearts and minds.

"But let us not forget our God is one of a jealous and vengeful nature. His followers are as Him too, also of a jealous and vengeful nature. This aspect of man must be acknowledged and dealt with. Many pretend it does not exist."

Barbara seemed to be delivering a sermon all of her own. It did not even seem to matter to her whether the two women listened or not. The sermon was going to be spoken anyway.

"It is due to His jealous nature, that He insists on being the One True God, that His followers in turn each insist they are the one true Church."

Barbara stopped for a moment... Then she continued, "Sacrifice must come.

"A portion of the wealth we receive from work will be given to the Church to appease them and allow us to continue with our duties here on the island. This will placate their jealous natures when they see us doing the work they themselves cannot do.

"It is said that we cannot talk to this God without the help of the priest, and so this God does not know the inner workings of women, and will never know what we say here. "

Barbara stopped for a moment and looked to Maria and Isabel as if expecting a reply.

"Innocence is never determined by the virtues of man for they will always have their own desires and perceive them as needs. Men are not Gods."

Maria and Isabel merely exchanged looks. "But this is Blasphemy" whispered Isabel into Maria's ear. But Maria seemed entranced by Barbara's words and looked toward Isabel and said,

"It is about men and women, and the church. And about giving. And other things I did not understand. But we should try to remember it regardless if we can. Many things Barbara says grow meaningful only later. Such are the many lessons she teaches us."

"Yes," replied Barbara,

"You are here to learn what is true and what is not. There is so much in this world and the other that will come to light very soon Isabel."

CHAPTER 3

The Priest

Padre João Cardoso had come to the house while the three had been out and made himself perfectly at home again, as he was often wont to do. He poured himself a tall cup of wine and sat at the table where Barbara had left some bread and cheese. He did not care whether it was his or not.

He was going to devour it anyway.

He heartily gulped down the wine, and began to look more and more satisfied as time went on. It was starting to rain on this side of Angra and the water spouts and gutters began to overflow.

The sound of water splashing was getting lost in the raindrops.

They will be back soon, he thought.. And he began to pour himself a second cup of wine.

If there was one thing he could always depend on in life, it was that Barbara had a plentiful stash of wine. Many people would bring wine to Barbara as a gift, a thank you for what she had done to treat their many ailments and to give out thoughtful and timely advice.

And if there was one thing Barbara knew about the padre, it was that he could always be depended upon to consume all the wine. Left to him, there would not be a drop to be found.

Padre João Cardoso was a man near thirty years of age, tall compared to most people on the island. His hair was dark and long but kept restrained in a ponytail. He had golden eyes that became the lightest color brown when the light hit them, as though God himself must look through them.

Though often, they were ringed with red from an excess of someone else's alcohol.

He was slender and always kept his facial hair shaved. And he was attractive to the women, though of course, he was not supposed to partake in the sinful pleasures of the flesh.

João was a priest at one of the many churches in the city and much to the dismay of his brother Gaspar, latterly, he had been devoting much of his time to Barbara's company.

So much so that the people were whispering about it, beginning to notice a lapse in his duties at the church. João was sure to keep up appearances when needed and tried to be discreet in his friendship with Barbara. But in a place as small and intimate as this, a place where everyone was in and out of everyone else's business, there was no chance of being successful at discretion.

He could hear Barbara's voice at the door.

So, they must be back. Hopefully, with food. Maybe a rump roast.

His mouth was still watering. Bread and cheese were rarely enough for a man.

Particularly not for a man who spent all his own money on women and wine to a point where he often went hungry—or ventured off in search of someone else's sustenance.

Soon, Barbara came inside with Maria and Isabel.

"Hello, Querida. How was your walk up the hill?" the padre said loudly with a mischievous smile. The odor of alcohol drifted across from his breath. His teeth stained red with wine.

Barbara was unfazed by his presence there and gave him a hearty slap on his shoulder for attempting to startle her. He would rarely succeed because he often did turn up in her absence.

Most likely, this was the preferred time for him to visit since he could help himself to everything in her cupboards. One time, he ate a whole pot of Alcatra on his own.

"It was good. We made it home before the downpour. How did you know we went there?"

"Ahh, I saw you walk past, but didn't want to seem impious by chasing beautiful women up the street," replied João with a laugh in his voice.

He often did chase women, a fact he seemed to overlook. Barbara ignored the fact too.

"Have you met Isabel? She is the woman I told you about."

João looked up with a sparkle in his eyes and Isabel came forward to give him a kiss on each cheek. "It's good to meet you, Padre," Isabel said. "I have heard much about you."

And she had. Much of it was an annoyance but she would not say that to him. She bit on her lower lip, having no reason at all to be annoyed about who came or went to and from Barbara's.

It was not her own place, and it was clear Barbara had a fondness for the priest.

Though she could not imagine why. He was not a man to her own taste, and seemed fickle.

"It is good to meet a woman blessed with talents such as yours," said the padre to Isabel, though he cast a nod to Barbara, looking for approval.

"Well, I truly am grateful to be here, Padre," said Isabel. "I have learned so much already, I'm honored, really Padre," Isabel said nervously. "I am learning from the best."

"We are all blessed by the knowledge we share with each other," Barbara cut in, "And young Isabel, you are very kind but be assured, I learn much from you too."

Isabel flushed. It was a nice compliment even if it surely was an untruth.

What could she, barely a woman yet, possibly teach to an old hand such as Barbara?

She knew nothing Barbara did not already know ten times over.

"Ladies, please, begin with your duties around the house and we will prepare lunch," Barbara said. "You do not need to be so formal around Padre João."

"No, indeed, you do not," the padre answered.

"Besides," Barbara went on. "The padre and I have much to discuss after his long journey abroad."

She made it sound so formal herself. Maria knew what *discussions with the Padre* likely entailed already. But Isabel still had much to learn in that regard.

And with that comment, Barbara took hold of Padre João Cardoso's left hand and led him to her bedroom and locked the door from the inside. Their *discussion* would begin soon.

CHAPTER 4

Feiticeira

Barbara's lover had left to pray the rosary and denounce his lustful inclinations before God. Their carnal relationship was something Barbara needed for her sorcery, something that gave her power, him being a servant of God in the form of a priest—albeit a somewhat wayward one.

His seed gave her power over the Church, and so, gave her fortitude in her work.

She would feed it back to him in his wine, supplicating him and bending him to her will.

His semen was a creamy white, the sign of a healthy and virile young man.

Mixed with her own fluids, it would make for a powerful connection to the priest, and to the powers of the Catholic Church, bringing her closer to God and igniting the powers within her even further. Barbara knew he broke his vows when he came to her, but she was a beautiful woman.

He was easily distracted by her graceful demeanor, her full breasts and unlimited wine on the table. Padre João Coelho Cardoso held a position at the church of Nossa Senhora Da Conceição in Angra, but he found himself in the company of Barbara more often than he found himself at church.

Barbara enjoyed João's inability to remain faithful to his vows since she took it as a direct correlation to her powers over him. But she found him irresistible as well, and to some extent, her connection to the priest was not purely to have power over the Church. She delighted in her priest's carnal sin, and in the attempts at secrecy it entailed.

They had a lustful infatuation for each other that could not be undone by the rules of the Church, or by any attempts of any churchgoer or do-gooder to keep them apart from one another.

Maria tried at times to dissuade her aunt. But the talk never went anywhere. Aunt Barbara would do as she liked, especially when it came to the ways of the flesh. The same could be said for the padre; Barbara even encouraged him in his waywardness, even though at times, she would tell him how badly he was behaving. But mostly, it was to tease and titillate him.

After all, which man of God did not enjoy a beautiful woman constantly telling him he was being a naughty boy? It was true to say they led each other astray, and with great pleasure too.

She still kept the Priest João Coelho Cardoso's seed in his own special bottle of wine, a necessary addition to control and bind him to her and to access his link to the Church from which she, despite all her stated 'wrongdoings' and sins with the padre, did not wish to be separated.

The connection also could never be severed for it would mean insanity for João.

Now, however, there were pressing matters at hand.

Word had come that a ship had sailed into the dock at Porto de Pipas.

It was her husband Pedro, coming back after a long journey across the ocean.

Pedro had been absent most of the time, gone to work on the ships, and relying on Barbara to take care of the home—and the wine supplies, something quite precious to him—while he was gone. He would often leave like this in the summer months, coming back and indulging in whores and wine on his return. Knowing he was about to show up again, her heart sank.

Barbara would build up her clientele and then quickly see them disappear when Pedro returned to the town. He had long since grown into an abhorrent and unclean man; no doubt the long stints at sea had taught him how to wear the same undergarments for weeks on end, or to not wash or never cut his hair. He never used to be this way. Not at first, when she had met and wed him.

Now, she might as well bed a farmer's scarecrow. He was so unkempt and abhorrent to her.

Not only that but also, his presence was a bane on her business, and utterly predictable every time he returned. An embarrassment to her and to God. She barely dared think of how it would be when the wretched man was back in the house. The only good thing about him was that he did work hard. If not for that, he would be under her roof all the time. And in her kitchen, sticking his nose into whatever she was doing in her preparations. Soon, though, he would be back in the house and there was not enough bitter orange, vinegar or herbs in the world to cleanse it of his filth.

***

Later that same day, she shuddered upon hearing the door rattle but she could already smell the grease of his oily flesh before she heard the sound of his repugnant voice. She swore she would rather go deaf than have to hear it and reply to it. What a shame he had not fallen over the edge of a ship or been swallowed by giant octopus. These things were said to happen to seafarers.

She waited and hoped.

But no, no such luck. Not the last time he had been at sea or this one.

"I'm home!" he growled as he forced open the door.

She had propped it with a large wooden chair as a forewarning in case he showed up sometime she was taking a bath, or, God forbid, in *discussion* with her padre. Not that a chair could stop a man coming in but the screech of its legs on the floor tiles would at least give a five-second warning before he burst into the bedchamber and pinned her down, taking what he believed he was due.

"Hello, my dear, welcome home," Barbara said, unsmiling and impatient. "I thought for sure you would have been lost at sea this time. But it's good to see you are all in one piece."

A bigger lie than that she could not even fabricate. Surely, it was plain to see from her face that she would rather not see him in one piece or at all. She would sooner his limbs had been scattered to the winds or drowned in the icy depths, to be devoured by sea creatures.

"Ah Pobrezinha" he said to his wife. "There was a moment when we feared we would be lost at sea. Like you say, the sea was not kind. But I am glad to hear you are happy for my homecoming.

"If that be the case, maybe you should open your legs for me. It has been a while."

He grabbed her breast and forced her against the wall, his roughened hands roving everywhere.

"Later, my love," she protested, though managing to don a fake smile.

"Oh? Why is that? Why not now?"

"I made you a stew, dear. Let it not go cold. Let us eat and sup. After that, *make merry…*"

She squeezed his thigh, feeling a shudder jolt down her spine.

Even touching him made her heave with nausea and revulsion. But she was an expert at feigning it. "As you will," he said.

With that, he made his way to the kitchen table where he could find a fresh unopened bottle of Aguardente and poured himself a cup. "You have been at my Aguardente again," he griped. "There was a lot more than this when I left. And the wine…where is the wine gone?"

"In the stew, of course," she said, looking big-eyed and as innocent as she could muster.

"What, all of it? You put barrel loads of wine in this stew? This here, in the pot?"

He looked suspicious and stooped to take a lungful of its aroma.

"Not that stew, specifically," she remonstrated. "But you see, every few days, I would get so lonely, my love. And I would hope that the very next boat might bring you in. So I made the stew for you frequently, just in case you showed up. I longed for that. I would put in the wine and then sit by and hope…and wait for you, my dear. And here I sit, having waited. Now, here you are."

She walked to the rear of him and planted a kiss on his greasy head.

After that, she wished to vomit because of the rancid fatty taste of his scalp. But instead, she took a mouthful of the stew. It did its job and removed the ugly flavor of his unwashed self.

Quite a hearty stew, though I say it myself, she thought. "Shall I serve you stew, my dear?" she asked, eyeing him as he tucked a napkin around his flabby loose jowls.

"I think so," he said. No *please.* No *thank you for making it.*

She heated up a bowlful for herself and pushed it into a dish which she set aside.

Then she added a whole bottle of strong red wine to the rest, stirring it well. Hopefully, he would gobble down the lot and then not have any strength to ravage her later.

He might even fall asleep and snore.

***

Pedro did not partake of more than a bowlful of the special stew, much to his wife's dismay. The wine had not yet dissipated and he did not wish to be too inebriated. Not yet.

So, he was only slightly drunk on a cup of aguardente and had but a bowlful of stew.

In this state, he was rendered mostly useless already, but not so much that he could not function. At this moment, he decided to go for a walk outside and soon found himself at the local whorehouse. Here, the whores looked forward to his homecoming as much as his wife appeared to. He was a predictable man when he was home, sitting in the chair, often drunk and useless.

He waited to be served hand and foot. This his wife did just to keep him quiet.

When he did decide to go out, it was most often to convince his friends and everyone else of how great of a man he was, to tell them where he had been on his exotic travels and to look down on everyone in the village for one reason or another.

Then he went to the local house of ill repute, and spent his money there.

Better them than me, Barbara thought. *Hopefully, he will die of syphilis.*

The venereal disease was rife among the whores and men of the town. It surely could not take long before he would show the dreaded pustules that indicated the worst was yet to come.

Barbara longed for the day she could say she was a grieving widow.

The widow part, she would be joyful for.

The grieving part would be because he'd have left her with nothing but his debts.

Because of this—because of his penchant for spending all of his pay on women and wine—she built up her business to be the best it could be.

And she worked hard for it. Barbara was not willing to give up her reputation again.

Certainly not for this lazy, filthy oaf.

It would take valuable time to build it up once more if he managed to take it from her; Pedro was sick in the head, and she often thought it would be a small mercy if he were dead.

But as he showed no signs of falling overboard, perhaps she had to deliver him a helping hand. After all, he looked to her to do most everything else for him. So why not this?

It would be like putting down a suffering and diseased dog that barked all night.

Good for the dog and even better for everyone else in the neighborhood who had to put up with the wretched creature pestering them and disturbing their rest.

" Maria!" Barbara yelled as soon as Pedro was gone.

"Isabel! Come!" Barbara frantically gathered ingredients for her new spell.

"We must prepare ourselves for what is to come," Barbara said in a hushed tone. "You girls need to help me. Hurry!"

"Help you with what?" asked Maria.

"What do you need?" inquired Isabel. "And what do you mean by *what is to come?*"

"Never mind that. You'll see. We need the head of a black cat. There are many down by the Port, so capture one and kill it by cutting off its head, then bring the head to me." Barbara said with nary a look up from her books in front of her.

Barbara's command left Maria in shock at the thought of carrying a severed cat's head back up from the port. And to think they had to decapitate it themselves...

"Won't people ask questions?" Isabel nervously wondered.

Barbara looked up from her work to Isabels face with growing annoyance.

"Don't worry about them. Do what you must. Take my sharpest knife, just keep the head in a sack and don't let anyone lay eyes on it. You understand what you must do?" Barbara replied.

Her stare was getting harder from mounting impatience.

And so, Maria and Isabel left for the port and did as they were told, soon coming back up to the house with a bloodied bag filled with the severed head of a black cat. It was a funny-looking thing, with tufted ears and a pointed nose. Maria had killed it. Isabel could not bear to.

While Maria had been gathering the cat's head, Barbara had already set about preparing a hole in the garden for the work they would soon be doing. The soil was rich, and moist, ready for whatever sowing need to be done with it.

When Maria had returned with the item, Barbara asked Isabel for a spoon which she duly produced. The two girls looked on in horror, exchanging horrified looks as Barbara carefully scooped out the cat's eyes, replacing them with fava beans*.

Then she placed the black cat's head with its fava bean eyes into the hole in the ground.

She covered it up with soil.

Over the site she prayed, both Barbara and Maria using their own blood and tears to nourish the ground and connect them to the spell.

"We will let this grow, and in time, this will grow into two fava plants. From that plant, we will each find a bean that will make us invisible to those seeking harm on us for what we are about to do." Barbara finished her prayer over the planting site. *noted in the trial.

CHAPTER 5

The Devious Plan

Padre João Cardoso had been the only one to know of Barbara's plan. He had come to her aid at the church when he found her weeping before the Virgin Mary.

"I understand your hesitation, Padre," Barbara said. "But in his will, he leaves money to the Church. So in the event of his death, you will perform masses for the rest of his eternal soul!"

"He leaves money to the Church? Are you sure?" the padre asked. His impression of Pedro was that he would not have any money to leave to anyone. He had observed for himself the man's drinking and womanizing ways. And he was quite correct. Pedro had nothing left.

But Barbara was not going to tell him that.

As far as she knew, her husband had collected together nothing but a mountain of bad debt, and whoever inherited that after he was gone would be most welcome to it.

She could scarcely walk about the town without one trader or other asking when her Pedro would be home. Their voice tone said it all. They might as well have said, *when is that thieving scoundrel of yours coming home to pay back what he borrowed from me a good five years ago?*

"It is better for the Church, better for all of us if he leaves this earthly plane soon, and your masses will assist his soul! He is of no good to this place and no good to me alive!"

"Take succor. It will be merciful. And I will be here for you, I promise. I will perform these masses, and I pray for your soul as well," replied the priest.

João embraced Barbara and as the next few minutes passed, he brought his face to hers.

He searched for something there; was there a glimmer of something in her eyes?

As the wind caressed Barbara's dark hair and softly cradled her face, João kissed her on her full lips. In the dusk sky flew the shorebirds laughing and cackling.

They sounded like evil children visiting from the tunnels of hell.

Perhaps the birds knew of Barbara's devious plan.

***

Her plan would benefit not just them, but the Church and community as well. Even if the man had no legacy to gift to the Church after he had gone, his demise would benefit the Church too. For one thing, he would not be around anymore to bad-mouth the Priest. And that same plan would salvage her reputation and sanity. João Cardoso even helped devise the details.

Barbara had been married quite long enough to this dirty beast of a man.

They had wed in 1634, and it was a tumultuous engagement.

In the beginning of her marriage to Pedro, when she'd still had hope for the future, she would pray her husband would stop his adultery and abuse towards her. At a certain point, she had been bruised and beaten. And it was at this point that the voice of Our Lady came to her.

Our Lady chose to guide her on what she needed to do to end his ceaseless mistreatment.

She now knew she must be bold enough to fulfill this prophecy given to her in her dreams.

She was not going to reproach herself for it because the guidance was divine.

A direct message from God.

So it was clear. Barbara had no other choice but to poison him with the fresh-pressed juice of hemlock, a plant that grew near the rivers of Agualva only at certain times of the year; she had been warned that it was poisonous and had a most familiar look to it, often being mistaken for the cooking herb parsley. She took the journey to Agualva, bringing back the fresh plant to add to her husband's food. She was now ready to make the preparations for his eternal rest. She would toil and labor over his last meal, with as much effort and love as she put into his homecoming stew.

She chopped the herb finely, stirring and mashing it to a point where the bright green juice was fully expressed and added it to the stew. She decided to add a small piece of lamb, one of his favorite meats for its fattiness and rich flavor.

Then she served it up with a giant ladle into the biggest bowl they had.

"You are not taking supper with me?" he asked her.

"No love. I made it for you. There is only enough sheep's meat for one."

He felt himself blessed; she could see it in his eyes. "You know how to look after me," he said. It was as close to a thank you as she was ever likely to hear from his fat lips.

In her mind, she said to herself, *and I know how to put you into a deep grave, my love.*

It did not take him long to succumb. He gobbled down the food like a man who had never been fed before. The fat dripped from his greasy chin. He wiped it on his sleeve.

Then he said, "You know, I do not feel so good."

Within an hour, he was cold and stiff on the kitchen tiles. She kicked him with a foot but could not move him. She poured aguardente into his mouth and throat so that he stank of it, careful to spill copious amounts down his waistcoat.

Then, the two innocent-looking young women helped to roll him into the yard, where they left him by the tall gate as though he had taken a fall after coming home.

In the end, it looked as though he had drunk himself to death.

"You see, I said there was something to come," Barbara said to *her girls.*

Now, all she would have to do was to explain to the padre why the drunkard's pockets had been empty after all, and how he must have gambled away the money that was supposed to come to the Church. At least, she assumed that he had nothing left to give. In the days to come, she would have to go through his meager possessions to see if there was any money left somewhere.

***

She wore black and falsely mourned the death of Pedro for three whole days.

It also took Barbara three days to sew the shroud for her dead husband.

She had prepared a needle for just this occasion, a needle blessed by her priest. She herself imbued it with her prayers for his restless soul to find peace.

The days after her husband's death became a blur.

She made preparations and allowed for space to have mourners come and view his corpse.

She had placed the washcloth in tepid water, and wiped it over his still body, bringing it to the water each time and going over the length of him, saying her prayers for each body part.

She placed him in his finest clothing, and wrapped him in a coarse fabric that she had made just for him, an expensive and tedious process where she had woven in curious and otherworldly items and signs. These were out of view to mourners, but in plain view for spirits on the other side.

It offered her protection from this horrid soul who had tormented her so much in life.

She sought to keep his spirit from returning, and bound his arms, sewed his eyes shut, and cut out his tongue for safekeeping.

She stuffed fragrant rue and hyssop into his mouth, to encourage his silence.

No one questioned his death. It had been well known that Pedro frequently enjoyed drinking himself into a lazy stupor and that he was frequently engaged in questionable behavior that would certainly bring misfortune into a home. He had always made himself out to be deeply religious, however. When she went through his things, she came upon a coin pouch stuffed to the brim.

As had been promised and was customary, he had managed to save a third of his fortune, leaving it to the Church as payment for masses to be dedicated to his damned soul.

But Barbara had been in mourning for a long time already, way before she helped him die.

She mourned the dreams she'd had of him, dreams of the man she had thought he was capable of becoming. She mourned her own losses—losses of the pleasures of the flesh she could have enjoyed with a man with more savory habits. Loss of belief that the good Lord could ever provide her a better man to keep. And loss of her own self in the course of her marriage.

It was certain that there was little left of the Barbara she had been—the happy and carefree one. Through his vile and obnoxious habits, he had managed to wear her down over the years.

Though this mourning had come way before his physical death, it was the death of the man she thought he would have been. But it was still grief.

Barbara was able to convey this mourning to the people, who looked to her with sorrow.

They gave her all the respect one would to a weeping widow.

Once the mourners had gone, Padre João Cardoso came to offer his final respects to Pedro and to visit Barbara. It was common courtesy to offer his respects to the beautiful widow.

Pedro's body was still on display in the home.

But Barbara was ready to engage in the final act of her spell with João.

"Come here, let me hear your confession," Barbara said.

She smiled with green sparks in her eyes.

"I confess, I am thinking impure thoughts. Animalistic thoughts," Padre João Cardoso said in a hushed whisper as he pressed closer to Barbara.

"Let me soothe these thoughts," she said as she brought him in close, and began to remove his vestments till he stood before her nude, exposing his erection that stood tall and impatient.

She slid her lips over the head of his cock and gently teased it with her tongue, hearing him moan. She felt at his balls, clasping them lightly as she pulled his member deeper into her mouth, the head of his cock now rubbing against her tonsils. He savored the moment as she increased the tempo, allowing her to work the motions till he could no longer take it anymore.

He began thrusting until his orgasm became apparent with the flowing of milk from his cock.

Barbara spat his seed into a cloth napkin.

Then, she carefully wrapped the cloth shut with some twine and set it aside while João reveled in the moment of afterglow. It was a little souvenir of their work tonight, and one that had, in the past, helped her gain control over her husband.

CHAPTER 6

Brother Priest

Padre Gaspar Cardoso had other plans for João. Gaspar was a stout man with black hair and dark eyes, and he bore an air of superiority from being in a place of authority within the Church for so long. Gaspar was a schoolmaster at the Angra Cathedral and had little time for dealing with the ideas of love. He was also well aware of Barbara and her illicit friendship with his younger brother João. The intimacy of the relationship was not lost on the people either, but no one dared to speak out against Barbara since her power over life and death was well known.

Indeed, Gaspar believed she had cast a spell on João which became evident in his lapse of duty within the Church. Barbara had to be to blame for it all. There could be no other explanation.

Gaspar could see that João devoted more and more time to the company of the witch Barbara.

João was a regular visitor at Barbara's home, where Gaspar could only imagine what it was they were doing—but he was quite sure it did not involve the Church or prayers or devotions.

Barbara was recently widowed, and it was uncouth for a widow woman to be engaging in relationships with men, much less a man of the cloth.

As his responsibilities were left by the wayside, João devoted more and more time to the company of Barbara. João relished their illicit relations, but also loved to drink Barbara's wine and offer conversation. Together, they shared aspects of sorcery, and God.

Gaspar had been increasingly frustrated at João's inability to focus on the task at hand, and sought to create him a new role as father of a church two villages away. João had obviously been getting worse and more cursed as each day went on. Their family had travelled to do the good work in these islands and create a life here. Brasil was chaotic, but there was much to do. Here, Gaspar truly learned the lessons of idle hands. Perhaps João would find more sanity when he has time to work on the matters of God and God only.

This move would help to remove him from the reach of Barbara.

The move would also have him reaffirm his vows to God.

CHAPTER 7

The Ritual

In the crevasse of Monte Brazil was a chamber lit by dozens of candles placed in small hollows dug into the earth on the side of the cave. The illumination was enough to see the faces of the men and women who came in search of help from the Sorceress. Before each person stepped in, João stood as the porter, dressed in his finest robes of opulent golden medallions and the best grade of wool.

He blessed each person, giving them a blessing and a small lit candle.

Inside, they met with Barbara, alone. Here, she gave them visions of their future and an opportunity to speak directly to God about their needs and requests.

Maria walked in, joining the chorus of lights. She could be seen from the outside, slowly making her way into the hidden portion of the cave where Barbara sat waiting. The wall had been beautifully illuminated by the light of the candles placed inside of the cave.

It was a beautiful, wondrous sight, heartwarming and welcoming.

In this place, Barbara blessed each person with healing, saying prayers and laying on hands.

This was a time of confession as well.

A person's maladies, she insisted, had much to do with something they had or had not done. Or it could be a family curse, inflicted to cause suffering.

Barbara made a mental note of each person's confession, making sure to take special care of those who had been harmed by another, and noting who had done what.

Prayers were offered to each person in the group, again led by Barbara.

Each follower received a small coin with a tiny cross on the metal, blessed to protect the holder of the coin after their confession.

This was to be kept and held onto, to continue the good work being done here in this place.

This was their easily concealed amulet connected to the continued blessing offered that night.

As Maria left the cave, she waited for Isabel to finish receiving her blessing, and the two walked together through the city, back toward their home. On the way, they listened to the voices coming through from the shadows and from the windows of the buildings above, mentally noting each sentence, word and feeling from this journey home.

They compiled it all and shared it with each other upon returning to their home fire hearth.

This guided them to a message for the work they needed to do, to empower the blessing from tonight even further. Departing the cave, the people all left in pairs without a word between the two, but having their ears open to the messages they might hear on the journey home.

Every word heard from the streets and doorways on their return trip was considered sacred, holding answers to their questions and offering a peek into their future.

At the end of the ceremony, Barbara and João were together, the only light emanating from the few stubby candles that remained. João slid one hand around Barbara's back, bringing her in close, gazing into her eyes. He held her, brought her body near to his with unquestioned mastery, and laid his lips on hers. Her body responded in kind as her senses felt every aspect of him.

This relationship she had with João was of a professional and sensual agreement.

They both felt drawn to each other, but both understood the abnormality of this arrangement. They knew that at any moment, they could be banished and separated.

And they too walked home in silence, listening to the gentle conversations coming from houses. At the crossroad between her home and the church, they separated with nary a look, both having a sufficient feelings of having done good work for themselves and the people who needed them.

Unfortunately, Gaspar had become aware of this procession, and waited in silence for his brother at the church. After a time, João steadily opened the doors to the church and began to move towards his bedroom when he saw Gaspar and two of his men.

"Why are you here so late?" João said.

He was clearly shaken by the presence of his brother and his men.

"I think you know why. I have been waiting for you for some time, João." Gaspar looked frustrated as he quickly made his way toward the trembling João.

"Do you not realize? You are making a mockery of our family and the Church! Your relations with that woman will end! This is not for debate, nor do you have a choice in the matter!" Gaspar roared, bringing his face close to João's. So close that João could smell his breath and feel his warm saliva on his face.

"You will cut all relations with *that* woman," Gaspar finished.

But João simply turned away, silent and defiant.

CHAPTER 8

Destruction

Gaspar had his men take João into the barely lit chamber within the Angra Cathedral. His men Manuel and Francisco placed him in chains that hung from the walls, his outstretched arms growing weak from the weight of his body, his feet barely touching the floor of the damp room.

He was covered only in a cloth wrapped around his loins.

His mouth had been gagged so he could not scream or speak.

But his eyes held the gaze of fear and pain.

"You have been seen repeatedly with the sorceress Barbara. I will be bringing her to the general vicar who will bring her under trial from the Inquisition," Gaspar proclaimed.

"You have allowed her to control your mind and in turn, allowed her access to the teachings of the church. It is immoral, I say, and God will wreak revenge upon you! Mend your ways."

Still, his brother João said nothing—even when the gag was temporarily removed to invite him to speak. He merely hung there, moaning and flailing in the shackles.

"This is just a sample of what they will do to you if you are included in this trial."

And with that, Gaspar signaled his man to bring the whip hard down on João's back, and with a cry, João took the whip as his back curled in pain. He was still intent on keeping silent.

He would not give Gaspar the satisfaction of knowing how deep the pain went.

This only piled more and more insult onto Gaspar.

He wanted to hear João plead. So he would pile on more and more punishment until João begged for his life to be spared, promising never to venture near the witch Barbara ever again.

"You are forbidden from seeing Barbara, and I will make it easy for you. First, you must suffer, for you are a sinner in the house of God."

Gaspar gave a final nod to the men and left the room.

"Let this be a reminder, should you wish to see your sorceress again," Francisco said with a smirk. He proceeded to grab the branding iron from the hot coals in the hearth of the room, and brought it before João's face. João, trembling with fear and shaking his head no, now began to plead with his eyes for him to stop. There were still no words from his lips when the gag was lifted to allow him to speak. And because there were no words of begging, the gag was put back.

But Francisco was unmoved and brought the hot iron to the middle of João's chest, searing João's skin and sending shockwaves of pain throughout his body. It was unbearable, and he writhed in his shackles, and tried to cry out, but his cries were muffled by the gag in his mouth. Manuel and Francisco took turns with the flogging of João, they made sure to not draw blood, but to hit him hard enough to cause the most pain, this went on for what felt like an eternity to João before Gaspar came back into the room.

Gaspar walked towards João, and cradled Joãos trembling face in his hands.

"I just want you to come to an understanding with me, this is merely a taste of what the inquisition will do to you if you are called forth as guilty. They have a habit of sending sorcerers to the Colonies as well, and they will confiscate everything you own to pay for the journey. Don't think for a moment you will go back home to *Brazil in comfort and luxury! *Genealogical research indicates that the Cardosos had initially come from Brazil to the Azores. Your family will be shrouded in shame for generations. Is this something you would like, João?" Gaspar asked, and João fervently shook his head no.

Gaspar roughly removed the gag in Joãos mouth and with his breath stinking of garlic and wine breathed hard into his face for a second and asked in his low baritone voice:

" Will you be speaking to or working with Barbara again???"

João took a few moments, which was too long for Gaspar and Gaspar slapped him in the face hard.

" I cannot promise that!!!!!" João Screamed his voice pleading with his brother.

"She has placed sorceries on me, I can no longer control myself!"

" Are we going to carry on like this João? Let me remind you, the Inquisition WILL come, if you do not commit to me now, you will be persecuted for your part in her sorcerous acts ."

With that Gaspar himself took to whipping João, he did not hold back the force of the whip and Joãos Back and legs began to drip with blood, as he screamed in anguish over the continued torture.

" Remove me from her! I will do what you say, please, stop"

CHAPTER 9

The Curse

Gaspar wasted no time moving his brother to the church one city over, he made sure any attempt at leaving would be resolved with physical violence. The Church was small but it was far enough away from the city that he would not be as tempted to visit the bed of Barbara. Once that was established, Gaspar found himself at the office of the General Vicar, the one who could help him rid the city of the witch Barbara permanently with his connection to the inquisitors in Lisbon.

Barbara took Isabel and Maria with her on a pilgrimage to the church of Sao Mateus where João served as Priest. The church was near the churning ocean, far outside the city. It was much smaller than his previous place the church of Nossa Senhora Da Conceição and had a more relaxed feel. She searched the grounds till she found him sulking in the shadows of the church, bent over some manuscript, his eyes dark from lack of sleep. He was visibly distressed when she laid eyes on him. He had been in prayer for some time and it took his eyes time to adjust in the light and have Barbara come into vision clearly.

"Please, I need you to go, '' João said painfully as his hands fell over the top of his manuscript.

"Why did you not tell me you were leaving? Why did you run off? Leaving no word?" Barbara said as she came forward and extended her hand on his.

João jerked his hand away and behind his back, his face full of worry.

"Your brother came to my door to bribe me with the money that I gave to the church, and he told me to leave you alone, that you are bored with me." Barbara continued.

"I need to hear it from you, why all this?"

"I'm hurt by all of this...All of it." Barbara said as she shook her head.

"All of what? I simply moved on, I need to focus on my responsibilities here, it is what I am meant to do, it is why I came to the islands." João replied

"You have found yourself in a snake pit! Gaspar has poisoned you!"

"Everything we have done together and you just dismissed me this way? You worked *with* me, I did not do anything but help you and guide your work within the church." Barbara Insisted.

"I came here to remove myself from your clutches, away from the temptation I feel when I am with you, I never worked with you, you cast your sorcery on me and destroyed my sense of will." João screamed at Barbara, his eyes red and face contorted into something Barbara had never seen before.

"LEAVE!! And never return!!"

And with that, João began to pray loud enough for them all to hear.

João continued with a litany of prayers directed at Barbara and her apprentices.

Barbara is angry, "He Prays for Chastity, to remove temptation and to expel evil from his sight! As if he never felt the press of my flesh against his! As if I am NOTHING!" She Screamed

Maria and Isabel grew nervous, not sure what to make of the situation.

There was no mistaking Barbara's fury from Joãos Dismissal. Her pain and hurt from his expulsion quickly became anger. Barbara stormed out of the church and down out onto the beach where she would find what she needed for her next bit of magic. * ~She released her hair from her kerchief and let out a mane that was long, flowing, and unkept, then she ran down to the shore. The wind whipped her hair as if untangling the energy within it, as she searched for the items that would serve her in her magic. She found a piece of flotsam from a shipwreck, rocks of a particular roundness that were smooth to the touch, she found green moss that had adhered to the rock wall just near the steps to the church. Out of her pocket she pulled out a coin and threw it hard and far into the churning waves of the sea. She yelled into the wind, cursing João and his brother for turning him away from her, but she vowed to bring him back to her. *From the original inquisitor's notes

She carried these items away from the church, and found herself at the home of her friend in Sao Mateus.

João had heard her voice in the wind, the scream itself was as if guided by the Devil. He knew what was about to happen, his mind racing as he ran out to the shore. The unforgiving and feral waves churned as if ready to regurgitate hell's most frightful monsters.

João could hear nothing but the shorebird Shearwaters call. A cacophony of laughter and screams, as if guided by Satan from the inner temples of hell. Joãos Eyes searched the shore, the noise was overpowering and unrelenting, destroying his focus He Screamed in frustration

"BARBARA! BARBARA! COME HERE!"

But Barbara was gone.

Piling up the rocks, she placed some of the driftwood in the center and got a fire going, on top she placed a cauldron, and got water up to a boil while adding the moss and driftwood to the boiling water. Over the fire, she is praying, unintelligible words. Isabel felt as though she had been put in a trance, as she watched Barbara, in a fury pouring her curse of João Cardoso over the fire. After Barbara felt as though the spell was complete and had done the work, Isabel saw her cast a coin out to sea, and they walked back to her home in Angra.

*Folk Magic noted in the Inquisitors files.

Barbara would not be taking chances with losing João. Any spell she could do to dominate and return him to her will be done, and Gaspar be damned if he got in her way. She would have them both under her power. Barbara was seen performing all types of rituals to encourage the return of João Cardoso. Not only was she obsessed with him, it had become personal.

CHAPTER 10

The Heart of João Cardoso

It was dark in the room, lit only from the tired embers that burned in the cauldron placed near where the two women were working.

Isabel watched quietly as Barbara gently brought the fibers of the wool and jute together on her spinning wheel, carefully spiraling the two into one united piece and then held each finished section in her hand and tied knots into it. When she had an acceptable knot, Barbara held it in her hand as she said these words;

*"I do not spin a string of tow, But the heart of João Cardoso, which I have in my hand"

Then she blew her breath onto them, and threw them over her shoulder to the waiting hands of Maria. As Maria caught each knot, she brought it to the iron cauldron of glowing embers and burned each one, each knot igniting in flame over the hungry coals. Barbara tossed each section of knots over her shoulder chanting the words over each knot until the spell was complete.

"I will not give up João," Barbara said as she tilted her face towards the fire. "no matter what threats or other actions Gaspar would take to keep him from me. He will come to me or he will go mad. There is no other way."

Barbara readied some string and thread and gathered the needle from the sewing of the shroud of her dead husband. She prepares a small cloth charm that she begins to sew into the shape of a heart, filling it with moss. One by one she takes 9 slivers of sharpened juniper twigs and impales the heart. All the while she repeats this incantation;

* " I sew thee with the needle of a dead man, so as thou may be mad for me, and only these words hear; the Devil entered the River Jordan so as to speak, and nine rods of juniper bring, and in the mill stone of Barabbas and Satanas sharpen them and in the heart of João Cardoso carve them, so as he may not be, nor wait, nor eat, nor drink until he speaks to me. " *From Inquisition File*

This particular charm was to be delivered to João at his new church, and once he held it in his hands, he would be compelled to come to her, or die alone of his madness.

Barbara could feel something wrong, there was a current pulling her in an opposing direction like a riptide, something attempting to drag her away from her work. Later in the night Barbara would have a vision; her grandmother would come to her dreams and gave her warning of betrayal, that Gaspar is actively working against her. It was time to take precautions as word of her sorcery was going farther than just the small islands they inhabited. By this time her Magical favas were just about ready for harvest. The next night she instructed Maria on specific work to put the beans into action.

Gaspar had found Isabel walking home from the market, her

cloak that she had wrapped around herself to attempt at some sort of secrecy had failed. He immediately pulled her aside off the narrow street into his home.

"Please, listen" he began

"I know you are new to the city, there is much more behind Barbara than you know, I am sure you have witnessed her work in Sorcery and that it is an abomination before God to do such things. If you are implicated, you will be taken away to trail and tortured. You MUST come with me and tell them everything you have seen."

"But I simply came to learn of the ways of healing and how to temper the spirits around me! None of this was my doing, I told Barbara to leave the priest alone, that it would put us all in certain danger!"

"Well, you know she implicates you as an accomplice, everyone knows you as such, and this will certainly put you in danger. You must testify against her at the trial or you too will be the accused"

Isabel was uncomfortable with the thought of testifying against her teacher, but this was not her plan on coming to Angra, it was not to collude with a woman intent on the destruction of a man, it was to offer healing and learn to control the energy coming from within and that which is around her.

"Think about what is said here, and how you wish to continue, I will help you"

and with that Isabel was led back to the dark and narrow streets of the city.

Night had begun to fall, the rain came down giving the streets the look of hammered tin. Isabel had returned to Barbaras home and found Maria and Barbara working on more sorcery.

"Isabel Come! I have an important lesson here, we need to protect ourselves from the evil doings of Gaspar, he is quickly becoming more of a nuisance than I wish. If we can slow him down, we can overcome him and the inquisitors" Barbara said as she gathered an image of Saint Erasmus and two lamps, then instructed further.

Isabel's mind was racing, thinking yes, yes I know this, he spoke to me. But she kept her mouth shut.

"Grab the 3 legged bench, and let us move everything outside by the garden." Barbara insisted, as she prepared for the working.

Barbara took her hair out of confinement, and slowly untangled each bound up piece one by one with her hands letting the rain wash over her and through her hair. The two walked down through the rain to the Garden and set up their space for the spell. *With the Image of Saint Erasmus Placed in the center of the 3 legged bench that they had turned upside down, they placed the two lamps on the side of the bench. At the foot of the image of Saint Erasmus, she placed a piece of paper with the names of Gaspar, the Vicar and João Cardoso. Then Barbara put the names under her foot and slipped them in her shoe as she stomped the ground, whispering under her breath a spell for the domination and subjugation of these men who have come against her. *Noted in Inquisition files. In this time of Portuguese magical history St. Erasmus is often used in Sorcery for violent domination. *Unbound hair was noted about Barbara in the Inquisitors files. This is indicative of the magical power of a woman's long, flowing and "unbound" Hair.

The rain abruptly stopped and the women stood together to pray, that they be watched over, that no one harm them, and to remove the evil that had attempted to control those around them.

Just as her vision had indicated Gaspar had gone to the General Vicar to accuse Barbara and her niece Maria of Sorcery. But the work of Barbara to return João Cardoso to her was not finished.

CHAPTER 11

The Magical Fava Beans

Barbara had been a woman who was well known for giving money to the church on a regular basis. She was also known to help people of limited means in the city with healing and other aspects of life. She was also well utilized by the wealthiest of the island and had kept her clientele's names and work secret. Barbara did talk to Gaspar, and let him know she would be giving his name to the inquisitors if he chose to say any more about her sorcery. Not only was he a client of hers, but the Vicars wife, and several other notable donors to the church in the city. These people would be under question, and it would be in the church's best interest to keep silent or their charity will be withdrawn.

Meanwhile the decapitated cat head fava beans had been growing nicely in the garden, and it came the time to employ their magical properties.

*Barbara instructed Maria to begin to stuff each bean from the fava plant into her mouth and when she felt the right magic of invisibility emanating from the bean, that was the sign that she had found the one magical fava that would keep help her to be invisible in the eyes of the inquisitors.

"When you find the right fava, you will keep it in this special pouch made from the altar cloth that was the only remaining item found unscathed in the church fire."

As such, she kept this bean in a special pouch, one lined with portions of the fabric of an altar cloth that had survived a fire that had been found unharmed in a burned down church. This was meant to keep their actions secret and help to avert any additional eyes to their practices. *Also noted in the Book of Saint Cyprian and inquisition files as a spell to create a magical fava bean that makes the practitioner invisible.*

Gaspar had brought Barbara before the inquisition and soon found out how unpopular he quickly became. Women glared at him and spoke of him in hushed tones, men avoided him in the street and in establishments, he soon found himself unwelcome in many homes and celebrations. He had no idea how much of a blow back could be felt from the community; people who had been regular contributors to the church's funds had threatened Gaspar that he would be cut off in the event of Barbara being found guilty of the accusations against her. Her influence over the people was strong, he had certainly come up against a sorceress of great power.

He did gather some supporters and witnesses, allowing for the Inquisition to do their work in recording what was seen by the people.

"I will tell them what I have seen" Isabel said clearly.

"As long as I am not brought forth in the trial or have anything to do with it any longer" she replied in a softer tone.

"Yes, of Course, Miss Isabel" Gaspar said with more confidence and now felt as though he had a case that could destroy Barbara.

A Note from the Author

Barbara was certainly a person of Influence and fame in the Azores Islands. She was a woman who brought forth the scrutiny of the inquisition twice; Once in 1652 and again seven years later in 1659. Barbara's work to return Padre João Coelho Cardoso back to her failed however and he has been marked as insane, and not much is known about him after that. Eventually Barbara had remarried a man named Henrique Lopez (1657) and was living on Rua do Galo near where what is now known as the *Praça Velha (Its was simply called "Praça" in the 1600s)* in the City of Angra on Terceira Island. Again, the inquisition had come to the conclusion that there was not enough evidence against Barbara for them to arrest and punish her or Maria. It makes you wonder, was it her sorcery that kept her from the clutches of the Inquisition or was it her cunning ways of Manipulation? Perhaps A little bit of both?

Original Document: https://digitarq.arquivos.pt/details?id=2318061&fbclid=IwAR0r AW2NaBFu8NNJq65IgTXycNBT5YLFsv10H81MMQFm7kI OO-0ge1EKtHA